Con

Cover illustration by Sami Sweeten

A catalogue record for this book is available from the British Library

Published by Ladybird Books Ltd
80 Strand London WC2R 0RL
A Penguin Company

4 6 8 10 9 7 5

© LADYBIRD BOOKS LTD MM

LADYBIRD and the device of a Ladybird are trademarks of Ladybird Books Ltd

Frank's *frock*

by Lucy Lyes
illustrated by Sami Sweeten

introducing the **fr** and **nk** sounds,
as in friend and pink

Fred and Freda's party was on Friday after school.

4

Their friends all came in fancy dress. They all looked really cool.

Fred was dressed as a frogman. Freda was a dressed as a bear.

Fred's best friend Frank was the only one not there.

Then at the front door there came a KNOCK! KNOCK! KNOCK!

Fred went to the door,
and Frank was there,
dressed in a frock!

The frock had flowers on the front and it was frilly and pink.

10

"Just look at that frock,"
said Fred, with a wink.

"But this is a fancy dress,"
said Frank

The Clip Clop Club

by Dick Crossley
illustrated by Sue King

introducing the **cl** **tr** and **gr** sounds,
as in clap, trip and grip

Everyone is busy
at the Clip Clop Club.

Clifford Clonk is giving Clara a rub.

There's Tracy Trubbs
taking Troy for a trot.

Busy grooming Greta
is Gregory Grott.

They are all set to go
to the Pony Show.

Clip, clop, clip...

Trip, trop, trap...

Grip, grip, grip...

Clap, clap, clap!

Auntie Kents

by Naomi Adlington
illustrated by Sarah Gibb

introducing the **nt** sound,
as in te**nt**

This is my auntie,
Antonia Kent

and some of the terrible
presents that she's sent.

She's sent a tent that has
no poles or pegs

and an elephant with
three front legs.

She's sent a plant that's
full of angry ants

and a pair of
giant underpants.

She's sent twenty empty tins of mints

and a set of all her fingerprints.

She's sent something blunt,

or bent,

or dented.

She's sent something that
she'd just invented.

29

So now, when I want
something pleasant,

I don't ask Auntie Kent
for a present.

31

phonics

Learn to read with Ladybird

phonics is one strand of Ladybird's **Learn to Read** range. It can be used alongside any other reading programme, and is an ideal way to support the reading work that your child is doing, or about to do, in school.

This chart will help you to pick the right book for your child from Ladybird's three main **Learn to Read** series.

Age	Stage	Phonics	Read with Ladybird	Read it yourself
4-5 years	Starter reader	Books 1-3	Books 1-3	Level 1
5-6 years	Developing reader	Books 2-9	Books 4-8	Level 2-3
6-7 years	Improving reader	Books 10-12	Books 9-16	Level 3-4
7-8 years	Confident reader		Books 17-20	Level 4

Ladybird has been a leading publisher of reading programmes for the last fifty years. **phonics** combines this experience with the latest research to provide a rapid route to reading success.

The fresh, quirky stories in Ladybird's twelve
phonics storybooks are designed to help your
child have fun learning the relationship between letters,
or groups of letters, and the sounds they represent.

This is an important step towards independent
reading – it will enable your child to tackle new words
by 'sounding out' and blending their separate parts.

How phonics works

● The stories and rhymes introduce the most
   common spellings of over 40 key sounds,
   known as **phonemes**, in a step-by-step way.

○ Rhyme and alliteration (the repetition of an
   initial sound) help to emphasise new sounds.

○ Coloured type is used to highlight letter groups,
   to reinforce the link between spelling and sound:

and the King sang along.

○ Bright, amusing illustrations provide helpful
   picture clues, and extra appeal.

How to use Book 6

This book introduces your child to common 'consonant blends' – combinations of two or more consonant sounds, such as gr in the word 'grip', or nk in the word 'wink'. The fun stories will help him* begin reading simple words containing these common blends.

- Read each story through to your child first. Having a feel for the rhythm, rhyme and meaning of the story will give him confidence when he reads it for himself.

- Have fun talking about the sounds and pictures together – what repeated sounds can your child hear in each story?

- Help him break new words into separate sounds (eg. p-i-nk) and blend their sounds together to say the word.

- Point out how words with the same written ending often rhyme. If t-ent says 'tent', what does he think s-ent or b-ent might say?

Some common words, such as 'some', 'said' and even 'the', can't be read by sounding out. Help your child practise recognising words like these so that he can read them on sight, as whole words.

Phonic fun

Playing word games is a fun way to build phonic skills. Write down a consonant blend and see how many words your child can think of beginning or ending with that blend. For extra fun, try making up silly sentences together, using some or all of the words.

My <u>fr</u>iend's <u>fr</u>og has <u>fr</u>eckles on its <u>fr</u>ont.